STAR WARS

USE THE FORCE!

WRITTEN BY MICHAEL SIGLAIN

ART BY STEPHANE ROUX AND PILOT STUDIO

Disney

LUCASFILM
PRESS

Los Angeles • New York

All rights reserved. Published by Disney • Lucasfilm Press, an imprint of Disney
Book Group. No part of this book may be reproduced or transmitted in any form or
by any means, electronic or mechanical, including photocopying, recording, or by
any information storage and retrieval system, without written permission from the
publisher. For information address Disney • Lucasfilm Press, 1101 Flower Street,
Glendale, California 91201.

Printed in the United States of America

First Edition, April 2015   10 9 8 7 6 5 4 3

Library of Congress Control Number: 2014937082

FAC-029261-15338

ISBN 978-1-4847-0464-6

Visit the official *Star Wars* website at: www.starwars.com.

SUSTAINABLE
FORESTRY
INITIATIVE

Certified Chain of Custody
Promoting Sustainable Forestry

www.sfiprogram.org
SFI-01054

The SFI label applies to the text stock

Luke wanted to learn the ways of the Force and become a Jedi Knight.

Luke flew his X-wing fighter to
a distant swamp planet.

Luke was looking for Yoda,
an old and wise Jedi Master.
Luke wanted Yoda to teach him
the secrets of the Force.

Luke's X-wing fighter lost power
and crashed into a giant swamp.

Luke and R2-D2 made it to shore
and met a funny little green alien.
The alien took them to his home.
The alien was Yoda!

Yoda didn't look like a strong
and mighty Jedi Master.
But he agreed to teach Luke
how to use the Force.

The Force is a special energy field
that can be used for good or evil.

Luke trained with Yoda
strapped to his back.

He ran through the swamps,
swung on slimy vines,
and even stood on his hands.

Then Luke saw a strange cave.
It was scary and cold and filled
with the dark side of the Force.

Luke took his weapons and
slowly ventured into the cave.

Luke was shocked to see
Darth Vader inside the cave!

Luke fought him and failed.
Then Darth Vader vanished.
He wasn't really there at all.
It had been a test from Yoda.

Luke still had much to learn,
so he kept training.

But there was trouble in the swamp.

R2-D2 beeped and whistled to Luke.

The X-wing sank into the swamp.

Luke didn't know how to get it out.

Then Yoda spoke to Luke.
He told him to use the Force.
"Do. Or do not," Yoda said.
"There is no try."

Luke used the Force,
and the X-wing began to rise.

Luke could not get the ship
out of the swamp.

It sank deeper into the water.
Luke could not raise the X-wing.
He gave up and walked away.

Yoda used the Force.

He raised the ship out of the water.

Yoda really was strong in the Force!
Luke could not believe it.

That was why he had failed.
He did not believe in himself.
He did not believe in the Force.

Luke trained even harder.
He listened to Yoda and
practiced day and night.

He learned how to use the Force.
He could even move things
with his mind!

While using the Force,
Luke saw a vision of the future.

His friends were in trouble.
Darth Vader had captured them.
Luke knew that it was a trap,
but he still had to save them.

Luke decided to leave
the swamp planet.
He said good-bye to Yoda
and promised to return.

Then he flew away in his X-wing.

Luke was ready to use the Force. He would save his friends and become the greatest Jedi of all!